KB078932

The Blank Puzzle

The Blank Puzzle
Hyun-Mi Yoo

Translated by Spencer Lee-Lenfield
Proofread by Ho See Wah
and Published 2023 by Hexagon publishing Co.,

ISBN 979-11-92756-21-9 (03810)

First Edition (2023)
Printed in KOREA
by
www.hexagonbook.com
joy@hexagonbook.com

Hosted by Art Center White Block
Sponsored by Arts Council Korea
Translation supported by
STPI – Creative Workshop & Gallery, Singapore

This book was published with the support of
"2023 ARKO Selection Visual Art"

WHITE B LOCK
ART CENTER

The Blank Puzzle

Hyun-Mi Yoo

Translated by Spencer Lee-Lenfield

HEXAGON

Foreword

This is a story for both young-adult and fully-grown readers.

Its main character, "Blank," is a blank white puzzle with neither a picture nor colors.

Blank is constantly confused about their identity, but keeps on dreaming of someday becoming one of the puzzles known for its "big picture."

As the other puzzles find their pictures one by one, Blank experiences all kinds of challenges and setbacks, but ends up finding their identity—and their dream.

Like Blank, we may well all be blank puzzles without

even a little bit of a picture to go by.

We all dream vaguely of finding our "big picture," and then fight alone for that dream, racing as hard as we can in the same direction everyone else is running.

As you, the readers of this book, follow Blank the pictureless puzzle, I hope you'll cry, smile, and in the end find yourself right along with them.

Table of Contents

The Blank Puzzle

When I wake up in the morning, the first thing I do is stand in front of the mirror and pore over every nook and cranny of my whole body.

I do this daily, though nothing ever changes. But this is my routine, and I never miss a single day.

"No excess weight relative to height, clear skin, well-developed curves"—

Pretty excellent shape, for a puzzle.

But my one downside is that I don't have a picture or colors.

Of course, I get by even without those things; it's no big deal. But from the perspective of a puzzle like me, it's an incredibly troublesome thing to have to worry about.

Maybe no one around me realizes I worry about stuff like this.

In front of my friends, I pretend not to care; I deliberately try to project an indifferent attitude on the outside.

But all the same, I've been trying so hard to fix my problem.

On my first try, I put my faith in a nutritionist who claimed "Your diet is what makes you complete," so I committed to eating green vegetables every day.

My skin grew even clearer and healthier; but unfortunately, I didn't turn green, and the diet didn't complete me.

On my second try, with the saying "There's always a way in a book" in mind, I read an entire book from the neighborhood library. There were a number of lovely branching paths in the book that I wanted to go down. But there was no way in it for me to get a picture.

On my last try, I tried praying to a photo in a barber-shop.

The photo was small, plain; but something about the words on it drew me toward it.

It showed a little girl kneeling and praying in the direction of a cross; on it was written, "Every heartfelt prayer comes true."

So just like that girl, I knelt down, put my two hands together, and prayed.

Were my prayers not heartfelt enough?

They certainly didn't come true.

Am I so spoiled for just wanting to be an ordinary puzzle with a picture, like all the other puzzles?

The See-Through House

Everyone has a first memory of some kind in their lives.

When I try to reach back for my very first, a blurry image crops up, like an overexposed photograph.

The first memory in my life was incredibly bright.

It feels gummy, moist, like a freshly snapped Polaroid.

In it, I was flying somewhere.

Both arms outstretched, like the pinions of an eagle, I

swirled and spun through the lofty blue skies.

The landscape unfurling before me was surreally alluring.

Clouds soaked in moisture, like overcharged watercolors, drifted plump and fluffy through the sky; from far, far off the roofs of villages, scattered in little lumps and clumps, looked like so many toy houses.

Bursting with joy, I cracked open my eyes just a bit, feeling the breeze tickle between my armpits as I glided along in peace.

But that wonderful memory ends there.

Because right after that, the little-looking roofs far below, with a *sudden fwoosh*, got much larger, racing toward me at a startling speed.

At that speed, they were going to crash right into me, I realized—

Well, damn.

And so I realized that I hadn't been flying; I'd actually been falling.

I just thought I'd been flying because I'd fallen so long from such a great height. I could see my real situation now, but there was no way to do anything about it.

I plummeted straight downward, like an eagle shot by a gun.

And when I next opened my eyes, I was inside the

see-through house where I currently live.

And because I've only lived here ever since, I guess this place is at one and the same time both home and hometown to me.

The see-through house is made entirely of some sort of shiny plastic in the shape of a cube. Though from the outside it looks small and plain, when you stand inside, it's unexpectedly broad, with a perfectly pleasant level of light and humidity.

A number of us puzzles live here together.

Though at first glance we may look more or less alike in shape and color, our pictures will all turn out different.

And in that respect, we each have different tastes and personalities.

So no two puzzles exist in the whole wide world that are exactly the same.

It's hard for puzzles with such completely different senses of individuality to live together.

But fortunately, most puzzles are pretty optimistic and considerate toward one another, so we get along, almost entirely free from the kind of common spats and quarrels that are a hallmark of life in most organizations.

But no matter how wonderful life here might be, no puzzle wants to go on living here forever. This is a kind of temporary residence, and as such every puzzle has to leave this place the moment they figure out what their "bigger picture" is.

We puzzles are ready to head out anytime, and all of us are hoping, praying for that day as we quietly wait in this house.

There is a single rule everyone must absolutely keep here.

Whenever a visitor comes looking for a puzzle, we must all stop what we are doing and line up in one spot, each at attention in first position.

A puzzle's "first position" means the pose that best shows off one's picture and overall shape. First, you lie flat on the floor so that your picture and colors face upward.

Then, face toward the ceiling, you stretch out your arms and legs as straight as you can.

And to make sure we don't overlap with one another, we keep a fixed distance between ourselves.

Even puzzles who are normally un-greedy and conscientious subtly jockey with each other for the most eye-catching spot in the center when these days come.

But I have no picture, and no colors, and so I slink off into an empty corner.

And I spread my flat, white, featureless chest toward the ceiling, and awkwardly do my best to hold the pose.

With so many puzzles all living here together, you might think that there would never be a dull moment, as if we were always whooping it up at a vacation rental.

It actually *is* like that, at least a bit.

But you can get lonely even in the middle of a crowd in this kind of "organizational lifestyle."

Because in the end, we're just co-workers who happen to have the same goal—not a real family.

Fortunately, I do have some particularly special friends, so I've never been lonely.

My friends are: Red Puzzle, Blue Puzzle, Yellow Puzzle.

Together with me, the Blank Puzzle, we hang out together like we're the Four Musketeers.

Red Puzzle is freckled with white specks over a red background.

She's fiery and brilliant, and the confidence with which she says what she thinks is palpable.

Her motto is "Faster, faster!"—so she briskly attacks

everything she has to take care of. But because she's always rushing, sometimes she does make some big mistakes.

Blue Puzzle has a wave pattern of some kind over a blue surface.

He's super strong and brave, as well as confident—almost like an older brother.

His personality is usually calm and quiet, but sometimes for no reason at all he'll suddenly let loose an enormous shriek—"KKHAAAAAAAANG!"—which remains a mystery to us all.

The baby among us is Yellow Puzzle, who has a long slash across a yellow field.

His warmth and gentleness make anyone who looks at him for long feel the happiness of a spring day at two in the afternoon.

But everything Yellow Puzzle does is horribly, horribly slow.

And because everything is so slow for him, he often gets frustrated. But it's really just because he's the youngest among us, and so his development's a little slower.

And last of all, there's me, the Blank Puzzle.

I don't have any particular looks or personality to put out there.

But other puzzles like getting along with me.

Because they stand out next to my pale background, I guess.

Everyone thinks I have an easygoing personality, because I'm quiet and I don't voice any strong opinions.

But I actually have a personality that's timid and easily hurt, even by small slights,

and I hold onto things deep inside me for a very, very long time.

White Marshmallow
on a Dark Sea at Night

I do have a dark history I'd like to forget.

It's connected deeply to my name,

"Blank Puzzle."

That's my name *here*.

When I first came to the see-through house, I remembered absolutely nothing of my past.

Worse yet, because I didn't even know my own name, the other puzzles just called me the first thing that came to mind.

So naturally, my name was just "Blank Puzzle."

Puzzles normally just call each other by their dominant color. Red Puzzle, Blue Puzzle, Yellow Puzzle, etc. But for some reason I got called "Blank Puzzle."

Whatever the reason may have been, I liked my name.

Every time the other puzzles called out "Hi, Blankie!" I felt happy.

Since they always said "Blankie" with kind smiles, I figured obviously it meant something good.

"Blank."

Not a common name, easy to say, just a little bit of a foreign quality. I was curious what it meant.

I thought my name might at least offer an important clue about me.

Up until I started school, I was full of anticipation and apprehension about my name.

When I learned to read, I'd be able to find out where my name came from, I thought.

But later, after I had learned to read and figured out what my name meant, I was deeply disappointed.

The dictionary definition for "blank"—which is wrong—says it means "empty space, devoid of anything at all."

But is that what the word *really* means?

What made me feel worse, though, were the other puzzles.

As I was figuring all this out, they started calling me the "Devoid-of-Anything Puzzle."

I knew I don't have any colors, or a picture, of course.

But all the same—did they have to make fun of that fact with my name like that?

Between the sense of betrayal and my own shame, I felt like my whole body was shrinking into an infinitesimally tiny speck.

I couldn't get to sleep that night, tossing and turning.

Were all those smiles they had once flashed at me merely masks?

I suddenly felt a sense of disgust at the fact that I'd once breathed in the same air as they had, felt like vomiting at the thought that the air they spat out was what I drank in.

I plugged my nose and mouth and stormed out of the house.

The nausea settled down once some of the outdoor air had entered my lungs.

The chilly breeze cooled off some of the fury I'd thought might detonate inside me.

I mean nothing to the other puzzles.

So from now on, they don't mean anything to me, either.

I decided to run away from the house.

But that was a rash decision, and I had no idea where I'd go.

Although it was the middle of the night, and although I was scared and uncertain there in the dark,

the thought of all those duplicitous faces they'd flashed at me came back to mind, and I clenched my teeth.

My hatred conquered my fear for me.

Running away from home was unexpectedly easy.

I walked for a while, and the first light of dawn started to rise.

It was as if the Sun itself was cheering me on this bold path, illuminating the dark road ahead.

It might only have been because I had nothing to eat and my stomach was empty, but my head felt ever clearer.

Around noon, the Sun had seeped down the crown of my head to enfold my entire body in its warming rays.

But by late afternoon, the situation started to shift bit by bit.

My shadow grew longer, my footfalls heavier.

I walked on, trailing my lengthening shadow behind me.

The Sun, too, seemed to have had enough, and slowly wilted behind my back, till it finally ceased to keep up altogether, and sat perched on the horizon.

And there it stuck fast, staring at me stubbornly, as if to tell me,

"This is as far as I got in me. From here on out, you're on your own. Be brave!"

Never before had I seen the Sun look so big or so bright.

I faced it, waved, and said goodbye.

The Sun grew soft in outline, like the yolk of an egg, and with a pop, dyed the entire sky in its orange glow.

That sunset was a farewell meant for me.

I sat there watching, not a thought in my mind, till it had faded completely from view.

When the Sun left, the whole world turned dark, as though a black curtain had fallen over it.

My arms and legs shivered and quivered, my empty stomach gnawed at my insides.

I am a puzzle with a soul. I can overcome any physical trial through sufficient force of will, I thought, trying to steel myself.

But without any heed to what I wanted, my two legs simply wouldn't budge.

For lack of better options, I sat down by the side of the road for a moment.

An intense wave of exhaustion overcame me, and I fell asleep sitting there.

How much time went by?

I awoke with a start to the cold autumn wind stinging my cheeks.

I tried to get up, but I felt dizzy, as though the ground was wobbling beneath me.

Maybe because I'd gone hungry all day.

But the work I had to do still remained.

One day, I'd have to show all the other puzzles who had teased me for being "devoid of anything at all" and gone around calling me "Blankie" that I actually did have a bigger picture.

Though I might die before that happened.

But till that day came, I would keep moving forward.

Then, though, an unexpected variable entered the equation.

As I lay there, drowsy, the night grew ever deeper.

I thought I might die collapsed by the side of the road

far from home. What an awful way to go.

Come on, let's get back, I told myself.

It's a well-known truth that sometimes big advances require a step or two backward first.

But then another problem cropped up.

Because it was so dark, I couldn't see the way home clearly. *Bam*—sudden terror gripped me.

But fortunately, in the depths of that darkness, from far off a faint light gleamed.

With that dim glow as a beacon, step by step I managed to walk.

The way back home was longer than long.

Only well past midnight did I finally reach the see-through house, filthy and exhausted in body and spirit.

But I just couldn't go straight in. So I waited.

My plan was to wait till all the other puzzles were asleep, and then sneak in without anyone noticing.

At the very least, I didn't want them to see how threadbare I looked after just a day of running away, then crawling back home.

But why on earth was every corner of the house lit up bright at bedtime like this?

Inside, every single light worth the name was on.

And no matter how long I waited, they all kept pacing around frenetically, very much not going to bed.

I got so sick of waiting there that I was close to collapsing on the spot.

Whether out of self-respect or something else, I just couldn't go on waiting any longer.

I lowered my head, lifted my weary legs, and eked my way ever so slightly into the entryway of the house. But the moment I came indoors, all the other puzzles breathed a huge sigh of relief and welcomed me back with smiles. They had been so worried about me that they couldn't sleep; they'd turned on all the lights like that so I'd be able to find the house from far away, they said. For just a moment, my sadness vanished, and when my two legs gave out beneath me, they clasped me to their chests and I broke down crying.

They were all surprised and embarrassed by my crying, but they didn't ask me anything. Instead, they sat me on the couch and covered my knees with a blanket.

Then they made me a mug of hot cocoa, with a sweet marshmallow bobbing up and down in the middle.

They stayed right next to me, quietly, the whole time it took me to drink it, in between sniffles.

There are inevitably moments in life when you feel completely alone in the world, and think everything is meaningless.

Whenever that happens, I set a white marshmallow afloat in a big mug of cocoa.

The mug's warmth covers my hands, the sweet taste of the cocoa enfolds my tongue; I slowly, gently close my eyes, and take a deep breath.

The marshmallow slowly dwindles down, like a shard of a glacier afloat on a dark sea,

and as it does, a small sweet comfort makes its way into my thirsty heart.

Nocebo

The flurry of chaos around my running away did clear up some misunderstandings with the other puzzles, and it was all over within a single day.

But I couldn't just get over the questions I had about myself.

"Can you call a puzzle like me with no picture a real puzzle at all?"

"If I'm not a puzzle, then what am I?"

Once I'd started raising these kinds of doubts, I couldn't stop the questions from turning into loops, as if they were biting their own tails.

I had gradually turned into a puzzle of few words but deep thoughts.

At the end of all this stewing, I went to see a puzzle expert.

On the expert's wall, a spray of puzzles with complete, finished pictures in neatly matching frames hung in a fluid arrangement. And on the desk, boxes full of new puzzles to be solved, stacked so high they almost reached the ceiling.

As I opened the door to walk in, the expert's eyes lit up, as though I were an especially welcome guest not seen for ages.

He was a middle-aged man, tall and lean, with a piercing gaze.

From the neck of his dark navy clinician's smock hung a loupe.

His appearance and dress looked so expertlike that I felt at ease.

"Do you know what puzzle I am?" I asked.

"Of course. That's my specialty," he replied. "We'll do some analyses of your materials, printing, and so forth, and you'll know right away what kind of puzzle you are." His voice was so big it seemed to boom.

"First, lay down flat right here."

His eyes glinted with determination.

He raised his loupe to the flat of my chest and pored over it carefully.

The eye of the puzzle specialist, who had brimmed with confidence, now quivered with modesty.

"Is something wrong? How is it that I don't have a picture?"

"Your material isn't ordinary paper... You appear to be a puzzle made of hard birch..."

"Hmm... So why do my sides look the way they do?"

The expert continued to mumble to himself, and examined my print, materials, and shape.

The results didn't seem to please him; the light in his eyes darkened.

Lips pursed tightly, brow knitted, he lifted his chin up high.

He was assuming the bearing and expression of an authority figure.

He held his breath for a moment and, as if pronouncing the name of someone very important, crisply and cleanly told me his findings at a slow pace.

"You are the first such puzzle I have seen in my whole

life. Peculiarly, you are a wooden puzzle, yet you have neither a picture nor colors; and your sides seem damaged. To sum up, you are an abnormal puzzle."

Anyone, even a non-specialist, could tell I'm not a normal puzzle. The expert confirmed this for me in his exceedingly awkward manner a second time.

He pressed on a small hollow spot on the left side of my back and whispered, as if sharing a big secret:

"This here is a scar from when part of a puzzle gets torn off. Naturally, the torn-off piece would have had more of a picture. If you find it, you might be able to figure out what kind of puzzle you are."

After hearing an expert verdict, I felt even smaller, shriveled up on the inside.

I knew I had some weaknesses, but I always felt good that at least I was a puzzle with a healthy, intact body. But in the eyes of the expert, I wasn't just a blank puzzle; I was also a partly damaged, "incomplete" puzzle.

I thought a lot of puzzles had a hollow spot on the left side of their backs like I do. But after the expert told me it was actually a scar, for some reason even being jostled there felt like I was sliced by a sharp knife.

That's not true pain; it's just a nocebo effect.

I tried to ignore it.

But for pain that had been fabricated by my imagination, it was awfully severe.

When I looked at it closely, it looked not just reddish but, worse, distended as well. And on chilly days, I felt like it was prickling and stinging me.

I tried to think positively about my scar instead.

If what the expert said was true, then maybe the piece that had been torn from me might have a picture. Just like a black box, storing my information.

But I couldn't find that piece anywhere.

Afterward, I developed a new habit.

I kept raising my left hand to the little hollow in my back.

That let me block the scar from view in a natural way.

If it couldn't be seen, it didn't hurt.

---

* ***nocebo effect***: the inverse of a "placebo effect," the "nocebo" effect happens when a doctor's negative words give a patient bad feelings, thereby wielding a negative effect on the patient even in the absence of other medical reasons.

A Happy Goodbye

Out of the four of us, it was Yellow Puzzle that found his bigger picture first.

I knew he'd been wanting to get a picture of any kind.

Whenever he had time, he'd go downtown to the puzzle shop.

He kept looking at the framed puzzle of a sunflower.

He would just stare at it, enraptured. "I'm obviously a sunflower puzzle," he said over and over.

But it turned out that he was a caterpillar.

That long slash in his yellow was the furrow between

a caterpillar's segments.

And then it all made sense, how slow everything he did always was.

Even his goodbye was very, very slow.

It started off as a breakfast farewell, but by the time he was done, it had turned into a dinner farewell.

We were all happy he found his bigger picture, but that meant that we had to send him off now.

The four of us squeezed each other in a tight group hug and had a good cry.

I cried so much my tears started to run into my mouth.

They were salty, but also sweet.

And so while sad, our farewell was also a happy one.

Back when we were the Four Musketeers, every time we played games together, we'd split into teams of two— but the other three of us always tried our hardest not to be on Yellow Puzzle's side. He was so slow that no matter what the game in question was, his team always ended up losing. So from a purely practical perspective, winning and losing were already obvious before we even started playing. But now, with just three of us left, unable to split into teams, we can't even play games as predetermined as that.

Wouldn't it be nice if Yellow Puzzle were still here?

I'd even be fine with being on his team every time.

One day, I missed him so much that I even went to look at the sunflower puzzle he had loved so much. It was a five thousand-piece puzzle, a print by an artist named Gogh. This large-format sunflower puzzle had been fitted into a space made just for it. The largest puzzles were displayed in golden frames with sparkling glass over them, and hung high on the largest wall.

I looked up at them, and complimented them as loudly as I could. "You're so cool. Absolutely perfect!"

They didn't say anything back, maybe because they couldn't hear me.

Worse, they didn't even look down; they just kept staring blankly off into space the way they had before, off at some place even higher.

What were they looking at?

I felt a little upset at their attitude, how they seemed to just ignore me.

The framed puzzles might look impressive, but in reality, there wasn't much to envy about them.

To be honest, at the end of the day, they were really just duplicates of more famous originals.

As soon as they were out of the box, they got put together immaculately, then fixed with glue and protected under glass. Then they spent the rest of their immaculate lives inside that frame, unable to venture so much as a centimeter outside it.

"Found it—I finally found it!" screamed Red Puzzle one morning, jumping boing-boing all over the place so hard that even the rest of us thought he had gone crazy. This time it was she who had found her bigger picture.

She told us the happy news in a flurry, then set about packing her bags with a womanly efficiency. Without so much as a word of farewell, she was off and gone before breakfast time had even arrived.

Her departure left a horrible void.

It was less the lack of a goodbye than it was the sense that something was missing.

But what?

Exactly.

She had left in such a rush that she had actually forgotten to tell the rest of us what her picture was.

She had worried about whether her picture would suit her or not.

But if it hadn't been right, she would have come back.

I missed her, but I still hoped for her sake she wouldn't

need to do that.

Fortunately, days passed, and not a word from her.

But after Red Puzzle left, I started to experience some odd symptoms.

First, I started to feel a tightness spreading across my chest, almost like indigestion.

My very core seemed to contract every time I thought about her, as if suddenly blocked up.

When I thought about it, I'd gone through similar symptoms even before she left.

Red Puzzle had exquisite, beautiful curves.

Her sleek red skin lit up everything around her.

She was full of confidence in everything she did, and always spoke her mind clearly.

I was always timid in bringing up any of my thoughts, mainly out of consideration for others, and so her self-assurance amazed me.

She was constantly attuned to what I said, and would guffaw at jokes of mine that no one else even bothered to react to at all, or even clap.

How happy that laugh of hers used to make me!

Hearing it brought me a joy like hearing Christmas carols in the middle of August.

All of this is to say that I would never hear that dazzling laugh again.

But as time passed, the pain dulled, slowly.

Time works on almost all pain.

But I was always curious:

"Exactly what was she a puzzle of?"

After Yellow Puzzle and Red Puzzle had left, the other puzzles, too, all found their bigger pictures, and eventually it was just Blue Puzzle and me that were left here.

It had always been lively and even rambunctious here, but with just two of us, it went almost silent.

Fear is worse than loneliness.

And by "fear," I mean the fear of being the last one left.

As if to cover that up, Blue Puzzle started acting even stouter and sterner. His overreaction made things feel even worse.

We ended up spending more and more of our time lying side by side on the floor of the see-through house, whiling away the days looking at the sky. Blue Puzzle would close his eyes, and, as if dreaming, tell me, "I think I'm a wave. A big, rollicking, blue wave in the middle of the ocean."

The reason was that sketched over his whole body,

there was a wavelike half-moon shape. I'd known this was an old dream of his for a long time. But I didn't think there was so much as a figment of a chance that he was a wave. That half-moon pattern looked to me more like a scale. But I didn't say so much as a word about this.

I just kept nodding along. *Yes, yes, I think you're right.*

Finally, Blue Puzzle got his chance, too.

He'd meant to go visit a picture of the sea.

He was standing in front of the mirror, getting ready to go out, when suddenly his face turned purplish, as though he was nervous. Quivering and shivering, he begged me to go with him.

I was all too happy to keep him company.

But as we walked along, water kept plish-plashing out beneath his feet.

He was so nervous, cold sweat kept pouring off him.

Clear, like water.

I wiped it away with a towel and kept walking by his side.

Who would have thought it would be the last time we were going to have a walk together like that?

In the end, it turned out the pattern on Blue Puzzle

wasn't a wave at all.

He was so disappointed, he couldn't say a single word.

On our way back, he started to plish-plash water out from under his feet again.

But this time, the water was a deep blue, as though some had smashed open a bottle of blue ink in it.

Distraught, he started crying blue tears.

I'd anticipated that he was going to end up disappointed, but I didn't realize he'd be quite this sad about it.

I felt a pang of remorse.

Maybe somewhere, deep inside me, I might have secretly been hoping he wouldn't turn out to be a wave.

But I hadn't *really* wanted him not to be a wave.

I was just afraid of being left alone.

Yet my sense of guilt about it wouldn't abate.

Placebo

Winter returned to the see-through house.

The cold was so sharp that Blue Puzzle and I didn't go out at all. Instead we just lay indoors, basking wherever the sunshine fell, as if we were laundry drying in the yard.

The clear glass on every side made the house perfect for sunbathing.

I tried imagining my body slashed across the skin by coppery beams of light. Me as a nice deep brown puzzle.

But no matter how hard or long I spent in the sunlight, even when my skin had turned so red it burned all night, come morning I went back to being blank white again.

I guess I was just naturally devoid of all melanin.

Maybe I was a puzzle with some kind of albinism?

Albinism is an extremely rare disorder that occurs when a congenital melanin deficiency leaves the body completely white.

When you have it, no matter how long you spend in the sun, you don't turn any browner. And worse yet, the lack of melanin leaves the body at an elevated risk of skin cancer.

Once I started suspecting something, I couldn't think about anything else until it had been resolved.

I found a dermatologist right away.

A plump little lady doctor in a bright sweater.

I sat straight across from her, asking questions with an expression of sober concern.

"Doctor, my skin is completely blank white. Could I be an albino puzzle?"

As if surprised by my question, she stared at me with wide, round eyes.

"Your skin *is* quite white. But seeing as how there's

nothing especially wrong with it—where should we start looking?"

She took my temperature, weight, height. Then she peered deep into my eyes, shone a light into the depths of my ears, pressed my tongue down with a cold metal rod so she could look at my uvula.

After the exam, she smiled and told me, "You don't have albinism."

"Really? Well, that's fortunate... But why is my body blank white like this?"

"Not sure. I'm sorry, but I just don't know, either. But I do know that you are one extremely healthy puzzle."

I kept nodding my head along vigorously at what she was saying, but I wasn't completely at ease with any of it.

"But something's been bothering me lately. Is there anything you can prescribe me for that?"

"Blank, dear. Don't worry about it. I told you, you're fine."

"Pleeease?" I simpered to the doctor.

She hesitated for a moment, then pulled something out of a drawer.

"When you feel worried or anxious, take one of these, put it on your tongue, and wait. It'll help." The woman doctor seemed a little tentative as far as doctors go, but she was motherlike in her warmth.

I took the strip of white pills laid out side by side that she had pulled out of the drawer, and then went home.

I started sunbathing again. The light was warm, but I still found myself quivering from anxiety anyway. I suddenly remembered the pills the woman doctor had given me, and took them out.

They were pale and flat, like aspirin, but had an odd hole through the center. I set one on my tongue and cautiously chewed. The moment I closed my eyes, a sweet mint taste burst across my mouth. The pill slowly melted, thinning out gradually. And with it, I could feel my anxiety vanish bit by bit as well.

This is known as the placebo effect.

The lady doctor had given me a piece of medicine-shaped candy rather than actual medicine. Though it did seem a bit like she was babying me, I didn't feel bad about it. I closed my eyes and inhaled through my nose as deep as I could. "Blank, dear, I told you, you're fine," I could hear her saying.

And before I knew it, the anxiety had receded and I felt calm again.

I guess what I needed wasn't treatment so much as reassurance.

At the very end of that long, cold winter, Blue Puzzle finally figured out his picture.

He was extremely embarrassed to say it out loud.

"I was a monster."

What he had thought was a wave pattern actually turned out to be the scales of a monster.

He seemed sorely disappointed about the fact that he wasn't the wave he'd wanted so much to be. Out of breath, Blue Puzzle panted out his farewell to me—"Bye bye, Blankie"—and then let out a gargantuan ululation: "KKHAAANG!"

It was as though he were screaming out of sadness—over leaving me here alone, for certain,

but also out of his deep regret over not being a wave after all.

Maybe it's disappointing to turn into some weird, awkward picture that's not at all what you spent your whole life earnestly dreaming you'd become.

And yet I was jealous.

Boy, it would be nice if I could see my bigger picture, too.

Or even just be any picture at all.

Whatever it might be, it'd be better than being a picture of nothing at all.

Just as I'd dreaded, I'd ended up being the very last puzzle left here.

Being completely alone made everything different.

Now, the see-through house felt so big it was too taxing to do anything in it.

Those bright windows were suddenly too shiny, that cozy air suddenly chilled over.

And the most different thing of all was time.

It was as if all the times when I'd come back so busy I could hardly keep my eyes open had suddenly come to a standstill, staringly numbly off into space as if spread out on a rack.

Even the bed where I spent every night dreaming felt uncanny to me.

It was so quiet at night that I could hear my breath, the beating of my heart.

When I couldn't get to sleep, I tried lying face down, then on my back, and kept switching back and forth.

And flipping back and forth like that isn't especially good for puzzles, with our flat bodies.

Every time I turned over, there was a little popping sound—*tock!*—and suddenly with a jolt that shook the floor I'd be jerked out of sleep again.

I wondered if it was because I slept with the door

open. So I got up to lock it.

But there was no door. The walls and ceiling had disappeared, too.

Someone had taken away the entire see-through house.

Since all the other puzzles had found their bigger pictures, there wasn't any need for it anymore.

I thought I might cry for a moment, but I swallowed my tears and tried hard to keep quiet.

My see-through house had been as clear as glass, yet hard as iron.

It might have been a beat-up old building made of plastic, but it was always pleasant and safe.

Even after an earthquake a few years back when some other large structures had hit it, the see-through house barely had a scratch on it. And when the monsoon brought storms that flooded villages nearby, it had kept us not just safe from the rising waters, but comfortably dry as well.

The UFO that Came for Me

I was sitting on the ground staring off into space, brooding over memories of the happy place the see-through house had used to be, when suddenly the *voo-IING* sound of an engine approached out of nowhere. I could feel a strange current of air around me. I looked up at the place the noise seemed to come from and saw a round, flat silvery object swirling and twirling as it hovered in one spot.

Like a UFO making an emergency landing.

It kept flashing a yellow-green light at me, as if blinking out Morse code.

As though it were trying to tell me something.

I stared at it, entranced, not daring to move an inch.

Were they aliens from my home who had come look-ing for me?

For some time, I had entertained the possibility that I might be an alien. Which would explain why I, as a puzzle from outer space, would be totally different from the Earth puzzles.

The round aircraft spun as if whirling through a waltz, drawing toward me with agility and grace. As it approached, something magical happened to me. My feet fell away from the ground as if in gravity-free space, and like a black hole the craft sucked me into it, togeth-er with even the dirt and dust around me.

Still coughing and breathless from the blurry, dense cloud of dust, I realized I had entered the inside of the ship.

Though it was pitch-black everywhere and I couldn't see a thing, something soft-textured and cozy enfold-ing my entire body was comforting me. It felt like be-ing wrapped inside a warm, plush, duck-down duvet. I felt like a vagabond returning home after roaming the whole world.

The combination of extreme fatigue and coziness seemed to shut my eyes for me; I plunged straight into a deep sleep. A sweet, long, deep sleep.

I felt light as air, as if all my exhaustion had flitted away and my body was left afloat.

I was excited and curious about this new home of mine.

But something was odd.

Why isn't daytime brighter here?

Unsure if I were still asleep or not, I tried hard to blink.

I was definitely awake. But I couldn't see anything at all, just like before.

I waited for my eyes to adjust to the dark.

After a long, long time, the blurry silhouettes of things around me started to emerge. I reached out to touch them, and realized what they were.

Oh, dear.

The thing I'd thought had been a fluffy down blanket was actually a big, revolting lump of lint. It was full of hair, the dried husks of dead bugs, and who knows what

other trash all jumbled and scrunched together in a re-
pulsive heap.

The UFO-like spacecraft was really just a big robot
vacuum cleaner.

I was so shocked with the horror of it all that I broke
down crying.

My tears seeped into the dust and lint around me,
forming a substance that stuck to me like chewing gum.

I tried so hard to stop crying, but my tear ducts were
like broken faucets, impossible to turn off. All the little
pieces of grime and filth wettened by my stream of tears
kept glomming on to me, growing larger and larger.

So I transformed into a big, amorphous lump.

For a few days, I did nothing but sleep.

I couldn't really see anything, and moving even a little
bit was so hard that I gradually succumbed to the torpor
and just kept sleeping. Every once in a while, the vacuum cleaner came back with a deafeningly loud noise.

How long will this take?

I had no sense of how time was passing in this dark,
dark place.

It felt like maybe the vacuum cleaner came back once
a day or so?

And if so, then about a week had gone by.

Every day, bit by bit, a little more dust and lint came in, and I could feel my throat tighten.

It made my head itch, and I tried to scratch it, but it was hard even to move my arms.

And the big ball of gray dust that kept sticking to me had started to make me look like an enormous caterpillar.

Kafka's *Metamorphosis* came to mind.

The protagonist, Gregor, one day suddenly turns into a gross bug, covered in slimy goo.

He was once a doughty son responsible for his family's livelihood, but that morning his existence becomes a burden for his family.

Gregor eventually dies, squirming and writhing in agony, alone in his room.

After he dies, his family continues peacefully with thcir livcs as though nothing had happcncd at all.

I had been sucked into a robot vacuum cleaner for no apparent reason one random moment, and was now trapped, immobile, in an enormous ball of dust-lint clay.

I would end my days here alone, like Gregor,

and this cruel world would return to getting on very well even without me.

Now that almost all the extra space was gone, even breathing was hard work.

At the thought that death lay just ahead of me, my mind grew clear and tranquil.

The days of my past, in which I took up arms against a sea of troubles, flickered before me like a magic lantern, and was gone.

Looking back, I really didn't know the first thing about being a puzzle.

When I thought about how I never had a picture, and all the perfectly healthy puzzles out there that did find their bigger pictures, all the days gone by really did feel quite unfair, and a bit pointless.

In the middle of all that, the deafening roar of the robot vacuum came back, and a fresh layer of dry dust and lint came in.

I couldn't breathe.

It felt like I wouldn't be able to go on.

And the moment I gave up and closed my eyes, with a sudden sputtering whimper the vacuum cleaner stopped.

Without warning, a blindingly brilliant light shot into the darkness.

"Vacuum—full..." muttered someone's voice to themselves.

Maybe they were trying to empty it out.

I suddenly snapped back to consciousness.

I had the intuitive sense that this would be my only opportunity to get out of here.

It'd be curtains if I got swept into the trash can.

I didn't want to meet my end in the fiery pit of a trash incinerator.

Heat terrifies me.

When the vacuum cleaner got emptied out into the trash, I jumped like a frog, as far as I could.

I narrowly missed the trash can, and fell on the ground instead.

Success!

An elderly white lady in a maid's uniform scooped me up.

"What's this?"

Her gloved hands rubbed off some of the thick layer of silt and grime that had encrusted me.

"Oh—a puzzle? Keith will enjoy this!"

She carefully put me in her pocket.

The inside of the pocket was clean and smelled good.

I slurped up lungfuls of the oxygen I'd been deprived

of so long.

I was elated just to have some fresh air.

I didn't know just breathing could feel so good.

Why is it that only when everything is gone do you realize how precious it is?

I felt the sense of curiosity and excitement I'd once felt about the dust heap where I'd nearly ended my life surge anew within me about this brand-new world.

Where would we go?

Who was Keith?

Will he really like me?

The moment the elderly lady pulled me out for her grandson, he shouted with excitement.

"A totally blank puzzle? Wow! So weird!"

He meets me for the first time and the first thing he says about me is I'm weird? How rude is that?

All the excitement I'd felt deflated as soon as I heard Keith talk.

"Weird" is the single word I hate the most.

I've always been different from the other puzzles to the point where I'm weird, and that made me feel awkward.

So when someone tells me I'm "weird," it feels like

they're making fun of me.

But Keith actually doesn't seem to be making fun of me.

As far as the word "weird" goes, the thing that's actually weirdest is Keith himself.

I've never met a lifeform as weird as Keith in my entire life.

Keith's skin is dark brown, like a Black person's, but his hair is bright blond, like a white person's.

He's just a kid, but for some reason he's very tall, taller than some adults.

Maybe one day he'll be as tall as a giraffe.

"How did a boy with dark skin like yours end up the grandson of that white grandma?" I wonder, but I don't ask.

Not everything that exists in the world can be explained.

I mean, there's my existence—and I'm a colorless puzzle without a picture.

The Cool Puzzle

"The cool puzzle."

That's my new name here.

"Cool" means "awesome," "trendy."

Obviously, those are good meanings, but I don't feel any better about things.

I have my doubts about whether Keith actually means it when he says he thinks I'm awesome.

Keith's house feels, roughly speaking, like a warehouse.

There's a plywood table in the middle of the living room, surrounded by metal shelves mounted on the walls. Except for a bed, there's almost no furniture that really feels like furniture at all.

And the corners are full of recycled objects, like old paper and empty apple crates, that Keith's grandma seems to have brought back for him.

Keith likes drawing and making things; he either sketches graffiti-like drawings on those items, or sticks other odd scraps and fragments of stuff onto the boxes.

"Where should I put the cool puzzle?"

After making such a big deal about naming me, Keith had to figure out where he was going to put me.

In Keith's house, too, there were a bunch of puzzle boxes, and I assumed I was going to go in one of those. But Keith seemed to want to put me somewhere else.

If he went to the trouble of deeming me the "cool puzzle," was he thinking about putting me somewhere befitting the "awesome" label?

The best spot in the whole room was next to the window.

From there, you could take in the entire room, and also look outside.

Privately, I thought to myself that I really, really wanted to be put there.

But after agonizing over it for a while, Keith's eyes turned to a little fishbowl covered in a blanket of dust on the table.

Please, not the fishbowl, I beg you...

It seemed like there had once been a little goldfish living there, but due a tiny hairline crack in the glass, it couldn't be used any more. Now all that was left was a heap of pointless shells and sand. I'd be better off in a box than in there.

But that's exactly where Keith put me, with glee.

Something pricked my back when he set me down. "Ow, that stings!" I shrieked.

"Oh, oh, I'm so sorry!" replied a voice. I looked behind me and found a piece of scrap wood, jagged and black with rot.

That must have been what poked me.

The wood scrap, shocked by my sudden appearance in the fishbowl, looked mortified from embarrassment.

It apologized to me immediately and with great courtesy.

"I'm *so* sorry. Did that hurt a lot? I didn't mean to poke you! Please forgive me?"

It would have been polite of me to respond with magnanimity to such a gracious apology, but the whole situation was so aggravating that I just couldn't bring myself to tell the wood scrap things were fine.

As if to try to salvage that extremely awkward first impression, the wood scrap tried to introduce itself.

"I'm so happy to meet you! My name is Blackstar. Keith calls me that because I'm black and I look like a star."

He says you look like a star? That's ridiculous! I thought, and nearly said aloud.

For the life of me, I couldn't see what part of this moldy little plank reminded him of a star. It was just a moldering piece of wood.

Keith had dubbed me, a puzzle without a picture, the "Cool Puzzle," and he'd given this jagged, dark wood scrap the completely unjustified name "Blackstar."

He was obviously mocking us. Giving nobodies like us these lofty names was such a sarcastic move. I'd known all along he had to have a sadistic side, but I had no idea he would be this twisted.

I tried hard to keep my distance from Blackstar, but the fishbowl was so small that it wasn't easy. And because there was no one around but the two of us, one thing or another ended up getting on my nerves eventually.

And every single time it did, I spiraled down the same hole of wondering why, why we had ended up here together.

Did Keith have some special reason for confining us in the same room?

Blackstar was a dark, scratchy piece of wood. I, meanwhile, was a blank-white, sleek puzzle.

No matter how you spun us, we had nothing in common, really.

Blackstar used to be a decoration of some kind in the fishbowl. But now, rotting and warped, it really had no value as a decoration at all.

And then it hit me: did Keith put us in here together because he thought we were both useless?

I kept dwelling on the issue, but I really couldn't come up with anything we had in common, apart from being made of wood.

But later on, I did discover one more thing.

On the left side of my back, I had that scar from where something got torn off me. Blackstar had a very similar mark in a similar place, as though something had broken off it at one point.

Was this a mere coincidence?

After the puzzle expert pointed out the scar to me, I started walking around with my hands on my waist. That way, I could hide that spot from anyone who might notice it.

But Blackstar just went around with its scar in plain view.

On top of that, it didn't even seem to realize it was there.

Blackstar's total blitheness started to rankle me. Because every time I saw its scar, it gave me the feeling I was looking at my own.

I couldn't take it any longer. I said something.

"Hey, Blackstar... If you put your left hand on your waist like I do, you can cover up that scar in a way that looks totally natural."

"Oh, thanks for thinking of that. But I'm good!"

I didn't understand what that meant. I goggled at Blackstar in disbelief.

But Blackstar just kept chattering as if it didn't care at all. "Scars are just scars, you know? Maybe it sticks out a little. But everyone has a scar somewhere. I mean, having scars is like having knees, or ankles. So there's really no point in covering it up."

"Blackstar, that's crazy talk. My other friends don't have any scars."

"Just because you can't see them doesn't mean they're not there. Sometimes your heart has scars no one can see at all, right? And heart scars can hurt even more than the normal kind."

So Blackstar was claiming that *everyone* has some kind of scar?

And so there was no point in me hiding mine?

I scrutinized my scar in painstaking detail.

But to me it was still a gaping sore of a kind that only I had.

A Star that Doesn't Shine

From the moment we first met, Blackstar proved unable to spend a single day in peace and quiet. I could count the reasons why it gets on my nerves, but the worst of them is how it kept insisting it's a real black star.

At first, I thought it was joking. But no, it wasn't a gag.

I couldn't care less about whether it wants to live a life based on a mistake or not.

But it was so awful to have to watch it really, truly *believe* it was a real star, taken in by a total delusion.

Mistakes may be a kind of freedom, but over-the-top *delusions*—those are bad for your mental health.

As its only neighbor of any kind here in this fishbowl, I just couldn't keep waiting and see what would happen if I pretended to go along with this hallucination.

I figured I'd have to try to shake it out of this vain fantasy.

First, I considered my options for talking Blackstar—the most obstinate of true believers—out of it. I needed a persuasion tactic.

I started by trying compliments.

"Blackstar! You have such a great name."

"Really? Oh, thank you so much for saying that!"

Fortunately, it never seemed to suspect my real intentions. It bit the compliments hook, line, and sinker. Time to proceed to the next stage:

"And, I mean—your *name* is Blackstar, but what's cool is that you're not *actually* a black star!"

"What do you mean by that?"

I weighed carefully the expression on its fact and delicately, slowly, went on:

"Well, stars all shine light, but you don't shine at all. Right?"

"Right. I don't shine at all!" It nodded its head along in

enthusiastic agreement.

The moment I started to feel relieved that it wasn't going to fight me on this, it took a bludgeon to my common-sense approach:

"So I'm a special star! I'm one of the stars out in space that doesn't give off light."

I couldn't believe my ears. What kind of half-baked logic was this?

The delusion was way worse than I'd thought.

It was like trying to let the helium out of a balloon. If you tried to just set the balloon down, it would drift up endlessly into the ether until it finally burst from the change in air pressure.

"So you're saying you're an even more special star because you don't give off light?"

It nodded along like this was the most natural thing in the world.

My stomach purled in on itself. My patience had finally breached its limits.

"So let's say you're right about that. If you're a special black star that doesn't shine at all, am I a super excellent puzzle? Am I *special* because all the other puzzles have drawings and colors, but I'm the only puzzle that doesn't? The one single blank puzzle in the whole entire world?"

But Blackstar's round black eyes lit up, and it said, "Why, yes, that's right! You're a really cool blank-white puzzle!"

I suddenly lost my temper and flew into a rage. "Oh, so now *you're* making fun of me, too?"

Only then did Blackstar look a little ashamed of itself. "Why would I make fun of you? I think there's a misunderstanding..."

A long, awkward silence pulsed between the two of us.

After a moment, Blackstar looked at me with a serious expression and said, "Why do you think you're a colorless puzzle? I mean, you have a white color, right?"

It looked off into the sky, as if steeped in reminiscence. "Honestly, the moment I first saw you, I was kind of breathless. It was the first time I've seen such a perfectly beautiful blank-white puzzle—not even a speck on you! You're the neatest puzzle I've ever seen in my whole life."

At this unexpected praise, I suddenly felt tongue-tied.

And then Blackstar looked straight at me as I stood there, shocked, and told me matter-of-factly: "Blank white is the start of all the other colors. It can stand for purity and holiness. But the reason I personally like blank white as a color is simpler than that. I just think it's the most beautiful color of all."

When Blackstar said this, I lost all my words, spun into total confusion.

It was as if suddenly out of nowhere an enormous hammer had come flying and crashed down on my skull, and in the shattered shell of my head a giant whisk frothed my brains around like soft tofu.

It had never once occurred to me that maybe white actually was a color. I'd always thought white was just the absence of any other colors.

I'd had a complex my whole life over my blank-white skin.

Could I really be a puzzle if I didn't even have a draw-ing over all that whiteness? I wondered, full of doubts about my puzzlehood.

But according to Blackstar, maybe I wasn't a failed puzzle. Maybe I was a perfectly beautiful one.

And if so, was I now feeling something like confi-dence over being a "special, cool puzzle"?

I stood in front of the mirror, chest puffed out.

But the puzzle staring back at me was just the very same "flat, white, chestless" puzzle as ever.

The first time I heard Blackstar claim it was a real star, I wondered what kind of crazy nonsense it was talking.

But even if no one else could see it, the more I looked at its total lack of doubt about being a "black star that doesn't shine," the more I, too, started seeing it differently.

I ended up wondering if maybe it was right after all.

Had it brainwashed me or something?

During my first few days in the fishbowl, I was so upset. I felt like I was stuck again.

But as time went by, it turned out not to be so bad here. It was a bit like the see-through house, in that you had a good view of all sides.

In the see-through house, the sky looked square, but in the fishbowl it looked more roundish.

Because the see-through house had straight walls, everything outside it looked straight. But the empty fishbowl had walls that worked like a convex lens, and so the objects outside looked warped from within.

And the beautiful white sand on the bottom of the fishbowl flowed softly here and there around the empty clam shells and pebbles, giving it a kind of seaside ambience.

I lay on the sand looking up at the round sky, feeling a little like the main character in the film *The Truman Show*, who realizes he's on an enormous human-made set.

I just wondered if maybe, were I to escape from here, the wonderful, vibrant, real world outside would be waiting for me.

I didn't want to admit it, but contrary to my first impression, Blackstar wasn't boring or twerpy at all. Although he'd looked a little sheltered, his rough black color gave him the charisma of a rock star's leather jacket. And though I had no idea where he'd gotten any of it, he had a lot of knowledge about the world outside. Most of all, his great sense of humor meant that we could talk for ages, and I'd laugh like a maniac, rolling around on the floor giggling.

But Blackstar also had so many sharp edges that if you didn't want to get poked, you had to keep a foot or two away. I started from a fixed distance and approached cautiously.

We passed the time talking about this and that as we lay on the sand flats watching the round sky. We spent so much time doing that, that before you know it, we were best friends.

The Brown Puzzle

Keith's grandma got up in the early morning to go clean, so he had to do almost everything on his own.

He made breakfast alone in the morning, then went off to school.

I think he wanted to be an artist when he was older.

After school, he came right back to his room and spent the rest of the day drawing and making things.

I thought Keith had quite a degree of talent for art.

There was a plain but pure beauty you could feel in

his sketches.

But it was pointless for Keith to dream about becoming an artist someday.

I knew how hard it is to become an artist.

It's expensive, for one thing.

You need a lot of money, and time, in addition to the hard work.

And on top of that, add connections and luck, and only then does an artist get born.

Keith was tall as a beanpole, and because he was so young, he really had no idea how the world worked.

No one out there would refer to the way Keith scribbled all kinds of things on paper in slashes and dashes and stuck them on boxes as the work of an "artist."

If you want to be an artist, you need to have at least a bare minimum of art education.

But on the money Keith's grandma made, they could barely cover rent and food.

To them, pricey art supplies or personal art tutoring were like unimaginable tales about a far-off land.

The landlord came to press them on the late rent.

Keith's grandma had to take two weeks off work sick

due to flu, and she pushed off the rent.

She explained what had happened, and begged for another two-week extension, just a little longer.

They narrowly escaped eviction, but in the wake of what happened, I think Keith understood his own situation a little more clearly.

He realized that, in a situation where even rent had to be put off, it was a pipe dream to want to become an artist.

After that, he didn't draw or put things together anymore.

Which, when you thought about it, was the right thing to do.

Rather than keep using up all your time making completely useless stuff, it's far better to study hard and become a doctor, or lawyer, or electrician, or other jobs that feel more like jobs instead.

But an unforeseen problem came up after that.

After Keith gave up on drawing, he started giving up on everything else, too.

He wasn't exactly a model student, but he'd at least gone to class reliably every day. But lately, he kept skipping school, just lying around home instead.

He didn't even think of doing his homework anymore.

He just knocked his head against the wall and played computer games.

If I only saw *his* back, Keith's reality was filled with nothing but turned backs, as well. I think the computer games helped him forget reality for a moment.

If he got tired of playing video games all day, Keith sometimes turned his head and stared at me in the fishbowl. Once he started watching me, sometimes he'd get lost doing so for the next twenty minutes.

Nine times out of ten, it was because in his eyes, "Huh—isn't that puzzle a little weird?"

I wasn't delighted with the sting of Keith's gaze. And no one else had looked at me for a very long time. What was it that Keith, too, saw in me, the blank puzzle, that made him look at me so long?

At first, Keith's gaze was a burden.

But the more often he looked, the less I ended up minding.

Actually, I'd been quietly waiting a long time for Keith to pay this much attention to me.

For some reason, when Keith spent this much time looking in at me, I felt like I could read his mind.

I could just feel it, without either of us saying a word.

I mean, he was showing me interest.

How did I know? I just knew, that's all.

I used to feel nothing but resistance toward and dis-appointment about Keith, but I was slowly starting to feel something else. Which is not to say that I suddenly started liking myself.

At first, I felt uncomfortable with Keith. But all the doors barred shut to him were loosening my feelings a bit.

After a long time just staring at me constantly, one day Keith took me out of the fishbowl and carefully put me together on top of the table. After he'd finished, he adjusted the distance forward and back, looking for the best angle from which he could view me.

He took a brown paper bag, some charcoal, and some other drawing materials off a shelf.

He carefully stretched out the paper bag and started drawing something on it with the charcoal.

I thought he'd given up on drawing, but here he was with a relapse of artist-itis.

I had to stay completely still, holding the pose, not even a twitch.

Because I'm a puzzle made of thick wood, once I've found my center of balance, it's not that hard for me to keep it. But it's very hard for me to just keep standing still without moving at all.

And it got *so* boring, just standing there in one pose for such a long time.

So exactly what was the reason I needed to stand there for so long?

I'm a puzzle, not an inanimate object!

Out of annoyance, I pretended the table was vibrating, deliberately sagging.

Keith stopped drawing and propped me back up.

And then he threw himself back into the still life I'd spoiled all the harder.

I tried to take it a little longer, but soon I got fed up.

I took the vibrations from Keith using his eraser as another chance to fall down.

He sighed deeply, forehead wrinkling.

As if he'd given up on setting me up again, this time he just ignored me and kept drawing. After concentrating on it hard for a long time, he finally held up the paper bag, as if it were complete.

His expression darkened.

For some reason, he didn't like it, and he crumpled up the paper and threw it on the table.

Even at dinner time, Keith didn't come back.

He was such a shut-in that he hardly went out at all, much less stayed out late at night.

I got somewhat worried.

What's happened? Is he angry at me?

I regretted all those tricks I'd used because I was sick of standing up.

The paper bag Keith had crinkled up and thrown on the table was still there, all alone.

What had made him so upset with the drawing that he threw it away after hours of working on it?

I tried to flatten out the creased-up paper bag.

"Wow!" I couldn't help but shout. I got goosebumps.

He had been drawing a brown puzzle.

It touched me so much it took my breath away; I just stood there speechless looking at it.

This is what I'd look like as a brown puzzle.

I didn't even know how to put words to the feeling.

Is this what it means to be moved by something?

As I stared at the drawing, my formerly complicated feelings about Keith started to melt away instantly, like snow.

I waited for him, quivering nervously.

He only came back after it was very late. I was so happy I almost leapt with joy.

But as if he couldn't even stand to look at the table, he avoided it entirely and went straight to lie down on the bed.

His back moved a little as he lay facing the wall.

He was crying, silently.

I felt awful, too, but I had absolutely no idea how to make him feel any better.

The next day, I got up early and stood on the table waiting for Keith in exactly the pose he needed. I wasn't sure if that would help him at all, but I wanted to try to help him draw his picture.

But Keith didn't even get up until after midday.

Late in the afternoon, he barely managed to wake up, then went out without even eating anything.

He came in late again and went right to sleep.

And the next day, and the day after that—they were all exactly the same.

Several days came and went like that, until Saturday.

On weekends, Keith's grandma didn't work, so she and Keith could have breakfast together. She came to set the table and discovered the drawing on the paper bag.

"Keith, did you draw this? The drawing of the puzzle

is incredible!"

Keith just grumbled as if he didn't like her compliment at all. "Why don't I like it? You only think it's good because I'm your grandson, and you like everything I do."

"Okay, I get that. I'm your grandma, I do like everything you draw. But this drawing is *really* amazing. I mean, anyone looking at it would objectively think it's a beautiful drawing."

After she left to go grocery shopping, Keith took another look at the drawing on the paper bag. Maybe he was curious whether it really was an objectively good drawing.

And after he'd looked at it, as if pulling himself together, he started drawing again.

I was so happy I felt like jumping up and down.

As if I'd made a pledge, this time I modeled for him as hard as I could, no tricks this time.

The decision was easy. But actually doing it was a thousand times harder.

Not that I was complaining. But there are times when holding a long pose, even when the stinging from stiffness feels like you're being shocked with electricity, is really hard work.

But every time it did hurt, I thought of the *Portrait of*

a Brown Puzzle on the paper bag.

And I was able to hold out a little longer.

Because Keith was using recycled paper, I ended up being sketched in all kinds of colors and with all sorts of pictures on me. My favorite was a picture of me he drew on top of a vintage silk wallpaper.

Had I ever imagined myself as a puzzle with a European paisley pattern?

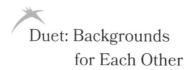

Duet: Backgrounds
for Each Other

I was so busy working as Keith's model that I barely had a chance to see Blackstar. After a long time, I finally had a moment to go looking for him.

Blackstar looked incredibly glum to me, after I'd been so distant from him.

"Hey! You rock star. When's your new album dropping?" I joked, hoping to soothe his feelings a bit. But that just made the vibes even worse.

It sounded like I was making fun of him.

I was only making a joke, but I was going to have to

fix it.

I lifted my hands and wriggled my fingers. Blackstar was so ticklish that even just seeing me do this sent him into uncontrollable peals of laughter. But as if he weren't in the mood, he twisted his body to avoid my hands.

And because of that, with a sudden *thwack*, I ended up squeezing my hands in the space left by the scar from the missing gap under his back.

From shock I tried to pull my hand out right away, but it wouldn't come out.

I was so flustered trying to pull it out that Blackstar at last broke down laughing. I burst out laughing, too.

Success, at any rate.

We laughed for a long time over that, the weird way I looked trying to get my hand back out of the scar.

I suddenly heard the signs that Keith was about to come in.

We'd meant to go back to our places after hanging out, but I couldn't get my hand out of Blackstar's back easily. And so that's the way Keith found us.

We just stood there, awkwardly, still connected.

Keith picked up the lump formed by the two of us and set us down on a bench nearby. And then, as if he were appreciating a great work of art, he slowly walked around the table. He took pictures of us from a bunch of different angles.

Then, thinking who knows what, Keith carried both of us over to the sink and poured some cooking oil on us.

No sooner did I have the time to think *What insanity is this?* then my hand popped, *bloop*, right out of the scar hole in Blackstar's back.

After Keith had prised us apart with the oil, he took us back over to the workbench again. He freshened up Blackstar's surfaces with fine sandpaper, then caringly cleaned them off with a soft cloth.

Blackstar's dark skin glowed an even deeper shade of ebony.

And only then did I understand why Keith had given Blackstar his name.

The first time Keith saw Blackstar, he must have seen this beautiful shade of black under the rotting plank.

A black so beautiful and deep, it was like it had sucked in all the other colors in the universe.

Keith varnished me with several coats of clear wax.

After that, my white skin glistened a milky hue. Keith stuck the two of us together again and set us on a stand.

Maybe because he was happy with the results, he stared at us with a glint of satisfaction in his eyes.

I'd only ever served as a contrasting white background for other puzzles.

That was about the only easy way for a puzzle with nothing of its own to get by.

But now, at last, I was a main character.

Blackstar helped give me the perfect black background to foil my white color.

His black and my white became backgrounds for each other, neither outshining the other.

We were partners in a perfect duet, both with lead roles.

The next day, Keith took a bunch of puzzles out of the bamboo basket where they'd been gathered.

At a glance, there was absolutely nothing striking about them.

Not only were they all mismatched in shape and color, but there were a number of puzzles that had wounds from being torn up.

Keith went about sprucing them up one by one.

He was conserving each individual color of the respective different-colored puzzles. He was also linking the hurt puzzles all together.

When all the spick-spackled, color-dappled puzzles were connected together in a round shape, it was just like a rainbow.

My tiny little impulse to make Blackstar feel better connected me to Blackstar, and then a lot of other puzzles.

Now, my scar didn't feel like it was just my own deformity anymore. I didn't care.

It had connected us to each other like a loop, turning us into remarkable supports for each other, each holding on so that the others didn't waver.

Keith spent over six whole months working constantly,

I was working as hard as I could to help him, too. Modeling is surprisingly hard, but because seeing all my transformations was appealing, I kept at it.

When you view a finished work of art, it looks elegant, but the hard work behind it is never elegant at all. Underneath the amazing form, there always lie patience and pain.

When Keith varnished me, the sandpaper he used to smooth out my sides hurt a lot. But to exaggerate just a bit: though those were the birthing pangs that gave rise to a new body, I took it without complaining. I felt a sense of satisfaction in all the hours I had gone through.

Even the stiffness and pain in my muscles made me feel good. I felt like I had a share of something in this world.

The first time Keith was fitting together the gaps in the different puzzles, he assembled and disassembled them like Legos to make the work he wanted. But after that, he tried a bunch of other different methods as well. Sometimes he made totally unpredictable puzzles out of glasslike or mirrorlike materials, or fused them together with everyday "found objects."*

They were completely different from any of the pictures or pieces I'd ever seen before.

One time, Keith hung puzzles in midair using fishing

---

* **Found object**: Means an item or thing that has been separated from its original, non-art-related use, and by being employed as a work of art, is given new emotional or symbolic value. Originally from the French term *objet trouvé*.

line, and they flickered like stars in the lamplight.

As they each twinkled with their own respective colors, the puzzles looked like a cluster of galaxies.

You could see Blackstar at the very apex of them all.

In the thick of all that radiance, his dark, un-shining colors had a space all its own. What he had claimed was absolutely right.

He was a unique dark star who didn't shine or give off light, and that really did set him completely apart from all the others.

When Keith called a black scrap of wood "Blackstar," or me, a puzzle with no picture, the "cool puzzle," I thought it was just a nasty way of teasing us.

But when I think about it now, Keith actually saw something in us at first glance.

In the black scrap of plank wood, he saw a deep and beautiful dark star, and in the pictureless puzzle he saw the possibility of drawing anything at all, like a blank piece of paper.

I think there are a lot of people in the world who go about wearing glasses tinted by prejudice.

Which is another way of saying that the world is full of unreasonable prejudices.

But what I didn't know is that I was wearing tinted glasses the whole time, too.

And so the world as I saw it was a dark one.

The immature person who kept warping everything through their vision of darkness—that was me, not Keith.

A Muse

But what would it be like if the whole exhibit were spoiled on account of me?

My heart started to race faster at the very thought.

But though it was just a small exhibit at Keith's school festival, to me it was the very first such event to happen in my entire life.

I was supposed to stand in front of other people and show them something—and the thought made me quake with terror.

I had a bad case of stage fright from it. I was so scared

I *wanted* to just run away.

But I wasn't *actually* going to.

At the opening of the school festival, everyone was dressed up their best.

Keith's hair was spiffed up with mousse, and he looked tidy.

And even if he hadn't, at more than two meters tall when you added his hairstyle, the image of Keith striding ahead confidently burst with model-grade handsomeness.

His grandma almost didn't find out.

She wore her only dress suit, a lilac two-piece with a matching hat of the same color that made her look as glamorous as Queen Elizabeth II.

I handled the stage fright as best as I could.

The whole way through the event, I kept my back straight, took deep breaths, and tried my best to keep my composure.

The students all enjoyed taking pictures for social media with the different works of art as backgrounds. I guess I *would* say this, but: out of all of them, we were the most popular.

They actually had to get in line to take pictures with

the puzzle art in the background.

Keith looked dumbfounded; it was the first time he had ever been so popular. And what's more, on the spot the owner of a little gallery downtown purchased one of Keith's pieces.

Keith put the money he got for the work in an empty glass bottle and set it proudly on a shelf in the living room. It looked like a trophy.

As if he couldn't believe it, he said to himself, "I actually sold a work of art, like real artists do."

After the festival was over, the other students kept posting their pictures with Keith's puzzle works to Twitter, Facebook, Instagram. They spread all over social media. Keith started uploading videos of the puzzle artwork and the creation process to YouTube. There's a shocking number of people on YouTube who really love puzzles, and after a month, Keith had over a million views. The local television station's flagship morning program, "Morning Today," heard rumors about the elementary-school puzzle art YouTuber, and sent Keith an interview request.

Early in the morning, the TV anchor and a camera operator visited Keith's house.

"Keith, I'm Chloe, and I'm an anchor for the live broadcast of 'Morning Today.'"

"Thank you so much. It's an honor to meet you!"

The anchor, with her long red-orange hair, was just as radiant and beautiful as she looked on a screen. She looked around the house at Keith's artwork with deep attention, eyes full of curiosity.

"Wow, there are so many pieces of puzzle art here. Drawings, paintings, and even an installation in the air. And you also combine the puzzles with other things, too? Incredible."

The camera operator traced out the anchor's line of sight, focusing on Keith's works one by one.

"This one is an absolutely enormous puzzle. And this one right next to it makes me feel like Alice in Wonderland. And what's this one? Oh! It's a puzzle made out of mirrors. So it shows my face in fragments when I look at it? What a strange feeling. I feel like I'm looking deep into myself, somehow."

Then she spotted Blackstar, too, at the very highest point in the ceiling.

"That piece of art, of the black star, is just amazing, too. Such a beautiful star."

She'd spotted Blackstar's beauty right away.

"The way you put the puzzles together is awesome,

but the combination of puzzles with other everyday objects is absolutely incredible. I'm just stunned at how you thought of all this."

"Oh, that's such a huge compliment, thank you."

"But Keith, your puzzles look entirely different from the average puzzle. You take puzzles whose shapes don't match each other at all and make them fit each other in a way that looks cool. How do you do it? Is there some special secret method that you use?"

"Haha, my secret is having no secret. There are no rules or anything for fitting the puzzles together. I just follow my imagination. But there's one rule that I do have. I have to try making something new every time. The new part is the most important thing behind why the art is interesting."

When I heard Keith's answer, my mouth popped open from astonishment.

Totally unintimidated by the camera, he sounded just like a real artist.

"I don't match the puzzles by their drawings. I put them together using my imagination, freely, and that's the way I make really new connections."

The anchor looked around thoughtfully at the works, and kept asking questions.

"Keith, something looks different in the way you connected the different pieces and puzzles in the rainbow. Why is that?"

"All the puzzles were hurt or damaged. I connected the damaged places to each other."

"Wow. So all those dented parts are damage?" she asked as she scrutinized the connections, her green eyes deepening.

She thought of her own hurts and wounds.

Don't other people just like her, who look fine on the surface, actually go about with wounds deep in their hearts?

"Keith, how do you keep coming up with fresh ideas for so many pieces of art every time? Do you have a special 'Muse" that gives you inspiration?"

Keith didn't have a ready answer for her this time. For a long time, the work on the puzzles had seemed just to flow from somewhere continuously, but every time it did Keith himself didn't even know where his imaginings had arisen from.

He didn't answer for a while, locked deep in thought.

The show was airing live, so it wasn't possible to give Keith that much time. Long stretches of silence looked

---

* **Muse**: A goddess in Greek and Roman mythology who represents an area of art or music. They usually give inspiration to artists.

like broadcasting accidents.

Everyone waited anxiously for him to answer.

After pondering the question, Keith's face suddenly lit up, finally having thought of his answer.

He pointed straight at where I stood on the table.

"The Cool Puzzle over there gives me my ideas."

The anchor approached the table, back bent, looking down at me.

As if flustered, her green irises quivered for a moment.

"This blank-white puzzle here, without a picture at all? This puzzle really gives you all your ideas? Really?"

"Yes, right. Like you say, the Cool Puzzle doesn't have a picture or other colors. So I can draw anything on it, like it's a blank sheet of paper, even when I don't have any ideas, and when I look at it the shape of the art just comes to me, like it's magic. Every time I just make whatever my imagination pulls me to make."

"Oh, wow. So this blank puzzle really is your Muse!" The anchor looked straight at the camera to officially introduce me. "Viewers at home! The Muse for this incredible art is this Cool Puzzle!"

The gleaming camera lens turned straight to me.

He said I was his Muse!

I was so shocked, the inside of my head went as blank and white as my face.

My throat tightened from the emotions. I couldn't cry on air! I held my eyes tight shut so I wouldn't cry.

The camera lens pulled in and gradually rested on a close-up of me.

Only now can I admit that I'm terrified of cameras.

The television screens were suddenly full of my blank whiteness.

Oh my God.

All the television screens had suddenly gone white.

I looked like a broadcasting mistake.

After the interview aired, thankfully, the art teacher at school saw how talented Keith was and offered him private lessons once a week for free.

I worried to myself about whether Keith, who had never taken a proper art class in his life, would be able to follow along in a dull basic drawing class where you had to start by drawing plain, simple lines.

But contrary to my fears, he actually really liked the lessons.

Keith would borrow big collections of famous artists' paintings from the library to study art history, and go downtown with other students to look at galleries.

Keith, who had always been on his own, suddenly had friends his own age. He made up all the classes he'd missed, and gradually did all the homework he'd neglected, too.

And just like before, on weekends he still drew on scrap paper and made art in peculiar shapes from scraps of "found objects."

He had started to dream anew the dreams he had once given up.

I used to think you shouldn't dream about anything that looks impossible at the start. I was so colossally wrong.

All Dreams Are the Same

From the time I was little, I'd dreamed of finding my big picture.

All the puzzles around me had exactly the same dream, too.

They had the big pictures they'd hoped for, like sunflowers or waves, but I didn't even hope for anything like that.

What choice was there for a blank puzzle like me?

I'd have been beyond grateful to turn out to be anything at all.

But it was actually pretty hard work not to be anything!

I was constantly scrambling to cover up all the ways I thought I wasn't good enough.

But no matter how much I loathed all my faults, I could never make up for them.

And that's the way I ended up living, for a long time.

All of that changed when I met Keith, who just kept on striding, at times plodding, toward where he wanted to go, without worrying about whether it was "not good enough" or "impossible."

I started wanting to try dreaming again about my big picture.

I closed my eyes, lay still, and tried to imagine myself with one.

But I couldn't see anything, even hazily or foggily.

Why wouldn't anything appear? Why couldn't I feel my heart spring to life that way?

Then, one moment, I suddenly realized.

Getting a big picture wasn't really *my* dream at all.

When I thought about it, I realized that becoming a big picture was the dream of *other puzzles*.

And from the start, that wasn't my picture.

So I couldn't even imagine what kind of big picture I wanted for myself, and my heart wouldn't jump for it.

I hadn't realized that the other puzzles' dream wasn't actually my dream at all.

For the first time in my life, I asked myself honestly, "So what *do* I really want?

I strained my ears to hear an answer.

I couldn't hear anything.

I held still and tried again.

I heard a quiet little noise, like the sound of a new-born crying.

I couldn't make out what it was saying.

No one had listened to me for so long, my inner voice had almost totally died away.

I stared off into space, overwhelmed.

Only now was I realizing I'd never even once listened for what I really wanted.

But when I did try to listen for my voice, my heart started to flutter a bit,

with a growing excitement and curiosity about what my future might be.

I asked, warily, *What do I really want to do?*, listening hard to my heart.

My heart's voice was thin, mumbly, a little rambling.

It had gotten so faint it was almost inaudible.

But when I strained to hear it, my inner voice got louder, bit by bit.

And one day, it will answer loud and steady.

Till that day comes, I won't give up listening to myself every day.

I am now flying in the sky.

Like the day I first came to the see-through house, I am flying freely somewhere high.

But this time, I'm not falling. I'm actually flying.

Which is to say—I'm taking a plane.

I look outside the window at the billowing waves of clouds below.

I miss Blue Puzzle, who had wanted his big picture to be a wave like that.

I lose myself for just a moment in that memory from the see-through house. When I look out the window again, the clouds have transformed into a vast, plush mat of quilt filler draping all the ground below. And now and then the downy filling scatters, and bits of grass and field poke through.

Clouds don't stick to a single shape.

I like that about them.

I watch how the bodies of the clouds flow with the wind when it blows by, and my heart leaps.

I want to be like a cloud, ever-changing.

Next to me, Keith wakes from a deep sleep, and after putting me in a see-through case, draws out a line and carefully hangs it on my neck.

We're getting ready to leave the plane.

Keith has graduated from art school, and is living as an artist.

He draws just as passionately as ever, and keeps on doing exhibits. And I have always been there together with him.

Whenever he has a new idea, he works hard to show those ideas in his art. It's fun, rewarding for me to do that work together with him.

I've been Keith's model and his Muse.

Our luck has been good enough for us to be invited to museums all over the world.

I've seen the country we're going to now countless times on maps, but I've never been there before.

I'm going to transform there into yet another shape.

Just like a cloud, always changing shapes, never rest-ing, always new.

Just thinking about it gives me chills.

Now this happiness—this is real, sincere, untrammeled happiness.

I've lived so much, and at some point I can't even say for certain, I started following the dreams I wanted.

I look outside the window again at the flocks of clouds already dissipating somewhere, and the little trees and houses popping up below.

The closer we draw to landing, the little houses get closer and closer.

We'll be landing soon.

I'm excited for what we'll see this time, and for the art we'll make there.

My reflection flashes for a moment in the window.

Inside the see-through case, my shape is that of the blank puzzle.

Same as ever, no picture, no colors, pocked with "defects."

For a long time, I had it hard because of those defects, but now they don't bother me anymore in the least.

Because I don't have any colors, I got to be a beautiful blank-white puzzle,

and because I don't have a picture, I got to be a Muse

that lures in the imagination.

As I passed through that long, hard tunnel, those defects forced me to realize their true value.

And now I can see my true shape.

I've always been a blank puzzle.

Author's Note

This novel is meant for young adult and adult readers alike.

When you change the frame of your thinking, everything else changes along with it.

Strip away prejudices and stereotypes, and you can see how valuable you are, recognize that what you have (no matter what it might be) is already amazing enough, and that those facts are more important than anything else.

The main character, the "Blank Puzzle," is a puzzle without a picture or colors.

As he goes about wondering, "Can a puzzle without a picture really be a puzzle?", troubled about his identity, he lives in pursuit of his dream of someday becoming one of the puzzles with a "big picture."

The other "normal" puzzles all find their big picture one by one, but when the Blank Puzzle is left all alone, he suffers the misfortune of being sucked into a vacuum cleaner. At the end of a string of trials and tribulations, he escapes into a new world, but is depressed to find the reality waiting for him is a trash can just as depressing and not much different.

In his new home, he meets a chunk of wood who claims to be a star, and the puzzle starts to think differently about his own identity.

The puzzle ends up helping Keith, a biracial boy from a low-income home, chase his dreams, and in doing so, the puzzle finds his dreams, too.

Maybe you, too, are living like the puzzle who's the main character of this book.

Maybe you dream vaguely of being one of those people who can see your "big picture,"

and are constantly running as hard as you can in the

same direction you see other people running.

There's never even a moment to think about what the big picture you want is, and in the short time you do have to think, you just have to keep running faster and faster.

If everyone else wants a big picture, then that must be my goal, too!

But if I constantly measure myself against that goal, I'll always come up short.

No matter how hard I flog myself to improve my deficiencies, I'll always be lacking something.

That's because I'm measuring myself using a ruler that matches other people's standards.

We may all be blank puzzles, each duking it out alone like this.

Is the place I'm rushing to get to really the place I want to go?

If I don't know my destination, am I just flinging myself toward wherever the light's on, like a moth toward the flame?

Does that mean I'm just listening to the voices of others, chasing other people's dreams, and ignoring the sound of my own voice?

What is it that I really want?

What makes my heart leap up?

What makes me happy?

I have to listen to my own inner voice.

It can sometimes be close to fading away entirely,

thin, mumbly, a bit meandering,

because I haven't been listening to it for so long.

But if I don't give up, and keep my ears open to what it says, my inner voice eventually gets louder.

And eventually at some point, it will speak to me insistently and cogently.

Keep listening!

The Blank Puzzle
Hyun-Mi Yoo

2023년 9월 7일 초판 1쇄 발행

지은이 유현미
번 역 Spencer Lee-Lenfield
번역감수 Ho See Wah
발행인 조동욱
편집인 조기수
펴낸곳 헥사곤 Hexagon Publishing Co.
등 록 제 2018-000011호 (2010. 7. 13)
주 소 경기도 성남시 분당구 성남대로 51, 270
전 화 070-7743-8000
팩 스 0303-3444-0089
이메일 joy@hexagonbook.com
웹사이트 www.hexagonbook.com

ISBN 979-11-92756-21-9 03810

주최/주관 아트센터 화이트블럭
후원   한국문화예술위원회
번역지원   STPI

이 책은 2023년 한국문화예술위원회 시각예술창작산실의 지원을 받아 발간되었습니다.